YASMIN

The Painter

written by
SAADIA FARUQI

illustrated by
HATEM ALY

To Mariam for inspiring me, and
Mubashir for helping me find the
right words —S.F.

To my sister, Eman, and her amazing
girls, Jana and Kenzi —H.A.

Raintree is an imprint of Capstone Global Library Limited, a
company incorporated in England and Wales having its registered
office at 264 Banbury Road, Oxford, OX2 7DY – Registered
company number: 6695582

www.raintree.co.uk
myorders@raintree.co.uk

Text © 2019 Saadia Faruqi
Illustrations © 2019 Picture Window Books

Edited by Kristen Mohn
Designed by Aruna Rangarajan
Originated by Capstone Global Library Ltd
Printed and bound in India

ISBN 978 1 4747 6555 8
22 21 20 19 18
10 9 8 7 6 5 4 3 2 1

British Library Cataloguing in Publication Data
A full catalogue record for this book is available from the British
Library.

We would like to thank the following for permission to reproduce
... Art and Fashion, ... paidaen.

TABLE OF CONTENTS

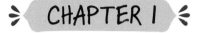

CHAPTER 1

The announcement

On Monday in an art lesson,

Ms Alex made an announcement.

"We're having an art

competition on Friday night! I

hope you all enter. The winner will

get a special prize."

Everyone was really excited.

Everyone but Yasmin. Yasmin

was worried.

She wasn't very good at art. Her circles were always lopsided.

And her hearts never looked like hearts at all.

"What's the prize?" Ali asked.

"That's a surprise," Ms Alex replied.

Yasmin frowned.

On Tuesday evening Baba came home with a box. "Yasmin, I have a present for you!" he called.

Yasmin ran downstairs. What was it? A new puzzle? A craft kit?

Baba helped her open the box.

"Oh," said Yasmin. "Paints."

"Yes, for the art competition on Friday. Look, there's an easel, and canvas too!" Baba said.

Yasmin wrinkled her nose. But she said, "Thank you, Baba," and took the painting things upstairs.

CHAPTER 2

Yasmin makes a mess

On Wednesday after school, Mama showed Yasmin videos of famous artists. There was a man with a bow tie who was painting trees. There was an old woman painting mountains.

Yasmin thought of her own messy, ugly artwork. She sighed. "I'll never be as good as they are."

Mama smiled. "It's OK, jaan. You only have to try your best."

But Yasmin still wasn't ready to paint.

On Thursday Mama said,
"Yasmin, finish your homework
while I make dinner."

Yasmin watched the video of
the man with the bow tie again.
He made it look so easy. She
decided to give it a try.

She set up the easel and paints
and tried to copy him.

A tree was easy,

wasn't it? No.

Maybe a little

flower? No.

Her pictures looked

nothing like the ones on the

video. Yasmin stamped her

foot in frustration.

Oops! Everything scattered

around her. What a mess!

Then she noticed something. Yellow paint had splashed on the top part of her canvas. She thought it looked like the sun.

She took some
brown paint and
splashed it on
the canvas too.

Then she
splashed some
blue paint.

Then some green
paint.

Soon Yasmin's
idea was taking shape.

CHAPTER 3

Competition day

On Friday night Mama and Baba walked with Yasmin to her school. It was strange – and exciting! – to go to school at night.

Ms Alex had decorated the hall with balloons.

"Welcome, children!" she said brightly. "I can't wait to see what you've created!"

Yasmin had a strange feeling in her tummy, like a hundred fizzy drink bubbles.

Mr Chen was the judge. He looked at Ali's mountains and Emma's basketball. He carefully studied each child's work.

Yasmin pretended to drink her squash. Mama squeezed her shoulder. "Don't worry. Your painting is beautiful!"

Soon Mr Chen tapped the microphone. "The winner of the competition is . . . Yasmin Ahmad!"

Yasmin couldn't believe it.

Her splotchy meadow painting

had won!

But wait – what was the

mystery prize?

A man walked into the hall. It was the painter from the videos!

"Yasmin, so nice to meet you!" he said. "For your prize I'll be giving you painting lessons next week."

"Thank you! But I have to warn you, I'll probably make a mess!" Yasmin replied.

The artist laughed. "Don't worry. I will too!"

Think about it, talk about it

* Yasmin doesn't think she's a very good artist. Why does she feel that way? If Yasmin was your friend, what would you say to her?

* What special skill or talent do you have? What special talent do you wish you had? Can you think of ways you could practise to get better at your talents?

* Some accidents are bad, but some accidents are good! Yasmin's painting started from a happy accident. Have you ever had something go wrong that turned out to be something good?

Learn Urdu with Yasmin!

Yasmin's family speaks both English and Urdu. Urdu is a language from Pakistan. Maybe you already know some Urdu words!

baba father

hijab scarf covering the hair

jaan life; a sweet nickname for a loved one

kameez long tunic or shirt

mama mother

naan flatbread baked in the oven

nana grandfather on mother's side

nani grandmother on mother's side

salaam hello

sari dress worn by women in South Asia

Pakistan fun facts

Yasmin and her family are proud of their Pakistani culture. Yasmin loves to share facts about Pakistan!

Location

Pakistan is on the continent of Asia, with India on one side and Afghanistan on the other.

Islamabad

PAKISTAN

Capital

Islamabad is the capital, but Karachi is the largest city.

Sport

Pakistan is the largest producer of handmade footballs in the world.

Nature

The longest river in Pakistan is the Indus River. A very rare type of dolphin lives there.

Make a flower motif bookmark

YOU WILL NEED:

- white card
- scissors
- ruler
- pencil
- coloured pencils

STEPS:

1. Use the ruler and pencil to measure a rectangle bookmark on your paper 5 cm (2 inches) wide and 15 cm (6 inches) long. Cut out the bookmark.

2. On a separate piece of paper, practise drawing the flower in simple steps, as shown.

3. Draw three or four of the flower designs on your bookmark, depending on the size of your drawing.

4. Have fun colouring your bookmark!

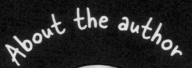

About the author

Saadia Faruqi is a Pakistani American writer, interfaith activist and cultural sensitivity trainer previously profiled in *O Magazine*. She is author of the adult short-story collection, *Brick Walls: Tales of Hope & Courage from Pakistan*. Her essays have been published in *Huffington Post*, *Upworthy* and *NBC Asian America*. She lives in Texas, USA, with her husband and children.

Hatem Aly is an Egyptian-born illustrator whose work has been featured in several publications worldwide. He currently lives in New Brunswick, Canada, with his wife, son and more pets than people. When he is not dipping cookies in a cup of tea or staring at blank pieces of paper, he is usually drawing books. One of the books he illustrated is *The Inquisitor's Tale* by Adam Gidwitz, which won a Newbery Honor and other awards, despite Hatem's drawings of a farting dragon, a two-headed cat and stinky cheese.